Note to parents, carers and teachers

Read it yourself is a series of modern stories, favourite characters, traditional tales and first reference books written in a simple way for children who are learning to read. The books can be read independently or as part of a guided reading session.

Each book is carefully structured to include many high-frequency words vital for first reading. The sentences on each page are supported closely by pictures to help with understanding, and to offer lively details to talk about.

The books are graded into four levels that progressively introduce wider vocabulary and longer text as a reader's ability and confidence grows.

Ideas for use

- Begin by looking through the book and talking about the pictures. Has your child heard this story or looked at this subject before?

- Help your child with any words he does not know, either by helping him to sound them out or supplying them yourself.

- Developing readers can be concentrating so hard on the words that they sometimes don't fully grasp the meaning of what they're reading. Answering the quiz questions at the end of the book will help with understanding.

For more information and advice on Read it yourself and book banding, visit www.ladybird.com/readityourself

Book Band 5

Level 1 is ideal for children who have received some initial reading instruction. Stories are told, or subjects are presented very simply, using a small number of frequently repeated words.

Special features:

Dinosaur words

Diplodocus
(DIP-low-DOCK-us)

teeth

Triceratops
(Try-SERRA-tops)

meat

Tyrannosaurus rex
(Tie-RAN-oh-sore-us rex)

claws

Velociraptor
(Vel-OSS-ee-rap-tor)

plants

8

9

Opening pages introduce key subject words

Large, clear labels and captions

Careful match between text and pictures

Big dinosaurs

Some dinosaurs were very big.

Diplodocus was a very, VERY big dinosaur!

Diplodocus

Diplodocus liked plants like these.

18

19

Educational Consultant: Geraldine Taylor
Book Banding Consultant: Kate Ruttle
Subject Consultant: Dr Kim Dennis-Bryan

LADYBIRD BOOKS

UK | USA | Canada | Ireland | Australia
India | New Zealand | South Africa

Ladybird Books is part of the Penguin Random House group of companies
whose addresses can be found at global.penguinrandomhouse.com.

ladybird.com

Penguin
Random House
UK

First published 2015
001

Copyright © Ladybird Books Ltd, 2015

Printed in China

A CIP catalogue record for this book is available from the British Library

ISBN: 978-0-723-29506-8

Dinosaurs

Written by Catherine Baker
Illustrated by Mike Spoor

Contents

Dinosaur words

Triceratops
(Try-SERRA-tops)

meat

plants

Diplodocus
(DIP-low-DOCK-us)

teeth

Tyrannosaurus rex
(Tie-RAN-oh-sore-us rex)

claws

Velociraptor
(Vel-OSS-ee-rap-tor)

A long, long time ago

Dinosaurs lived here a long, long time ago.

The dinosaurs are not here now.

All these dinosaurs lived
here a very long time ago.

Plants

Some dinosaurs liked plants.

Triceratops

plant

Triceratops was a big dinosaur
that liked plants very much.

Meat

Some dinosaurs liked meat. Tyrannosaurus rex was a strong dinosaur that liked meat very much.

Triceratops

Tyrannosaurus rex

meat

Look out, Triceratops!
Tyrannosaurus rex likes meat!

Little dinosaurs

Many dinosaurs were
very little.

Velociraptor

Velociraptor was a little dinosaur.
It liked meat, too.

Big dinosaurs

Some dinosaurs were very big.

Diplodocus was a very, VERY big dinosaur!

Diplodocus

Diplodocus liked plants like these.

Strong teeth

Some dinosaurs had big, strong teeth.

Tyrannosaurus rex had teeth that were VERY big and strong.

Tyrannosaurus rex

teeth

Look out! Tyrannosaurus rex's teeth are VERY big!

Big claws

Some dinosaurs had big claws.

Velociraptor had VERY big, strong claws!

Velociraptor

Look at the Velociraptor's
BIG claws.

 claws

Strong dinosaurs

Some dinosaurs were very strong.

Diplodocus was very big and strong.

Diplodocus

Tyrannosaurus rex was not as big as Diplodocus, but it was very strong.

Look at Tyrannosaurus rex's strong teeth.

Dinosaurs now

Come in here to see
dinosaurs now!

You can see many, many dinosaurs in here!

Picture glossary

 claws

 Diplodocus

 meat

 plants

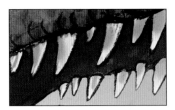 teeth

 Triceratops

 Tyrannosaurus rex

 Velociraptor

Index

Dinosaurs quiz

What have you learnt about dinosaurs?
Answer these questions and find out!

- ## What did dinosaurs eat?

- ## Which dinosaur had strong teeth?

- ## Which dinosaur had very big claws?

Tick the books you've read!

Level 1

Level 2